for Marshall,

Pokey,

and Mr. Squirms

CARROT
SEEDS

TURNIP
SEEDS

...ITS

Library of Congress Cataloging in Publication Data
Ernst, Lisa Campbell. Miss Penny and Mr. Grubbs/by Lisa
Campbell Ernst — 1st ed.   p.   cm.   Summary: With
the help of hungry rabbits, jealous Mr. Grubbs sabotages
the prize-winning garden of his neighbor Miss Penny.
ISBN 0-02-733563-1
[1. Gardening—fiction. 2. Rabbits—fiction.] I. Title.
PZ7.E7323Mi 1991 [E]—dc20 90-43175 CIP AC

Special thanks to
County Extension Agent
Dennis Patton

r of the
very large
productive
inches high.

be planted in
ll danger of frost
Started in-doors,
ted to the open
en weather appears
ld dug and liberally
dug with manure best.

THIS PKT. HAS BEEN FILLED
...NATION OF 80% OR BETTER
...FLT UP BY
...+C, S+W. LEE
...HVILLE, N.C.

MISS PENNY AND MR. GRUBBS

Lisa Campbell Ernst

Bradbury Press
New York

Collier Macmillan Canada   Toronto
Maxwell Macmillan International Publishing Group
New York   Oxford   Singapore   Sydney

Miss Penny and Mr. Grubbs
had been next-door neighbors
for forty-eight years.

And for all forty-eight summers, the same thing had happened: Miss Penny's incredible garden grew enormous vegetables—mountains of them—and Mr. Grubbs's garden did not.

Miss Penny was a familiar sight in Oak Grove,
driving her truck around town, delivering gifts from her garden:
carrots and beans, cucumbers, lettuce, and more. Her friends
all called her "the vegetable lady."

And every year, Miss Penny's vegetables won at the county
fair. Award ribbons lined the walls of her parlor, floor to ceiling.

Mr. Grubbs had few friends, and his measly vegetables
had never won a single ribbon.

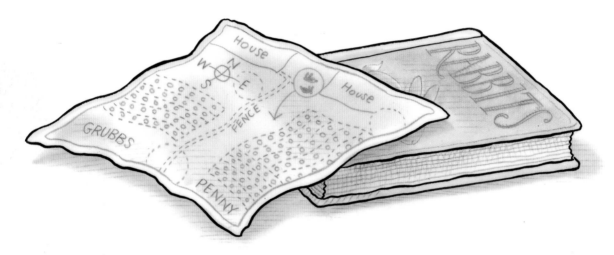

But Mr. Grubbs swore *this* year would be different. "I'm tired of her winning!" he snapped. "So tired I could spit."

All winter long, the vengeful Mr. Grubbs plotted and planned. By spring, he had devised the most evil scheme one gardener can plan against another.

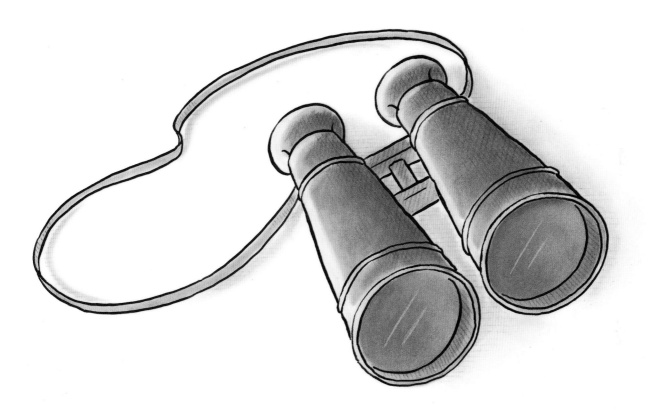

And then, Mr. Grubbs sat back to watch.

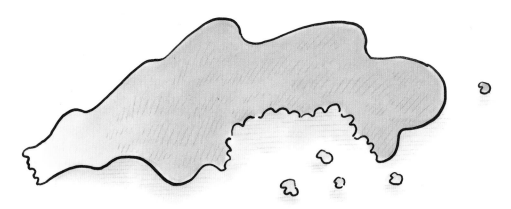

It took Miss Penny several days to notice that something was wrong. Weeding along a row of radishes, she discovered a small bed of lettuce, nibbled to the quick.

Miss Penny's mouth dropped open. She had read about this in her gardening books. "Rabbits!" she gasped.

Mr. Grubbs laughed himself silly.

"A fence," Miss Penny decided, and quickly got to work. Under the watchful eye of Mr. Grubbs, she brought out her tools and spent the rest of the day hurriedly sawing and hammering.

"Now *that*," she said proudly, "should keep my garden safe from rabbits."

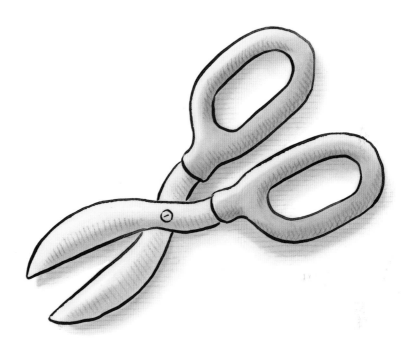

And it would have been safe, except for the scheming Mr. Grubbs. "You rabbits gained some weight," he gleefully noted that night, snipping through the fence.

The growing rabbits returned to their work with enthusiasm.
By the next morning, Miss Penny's garden was missing two rows
of broccoli and one of turnip greens.

"Jumping jelly beans!" Miss Penny cried, examining the
fence. "Those rabbits have sharp teeth!"

Shaken, she consulted her book about garden pests. First
she tried playing music all night; then making a scarecrow; then
even building safety basket traps.

But every night Mr. Grubbs made
sure her efforts were fruitless.

In fact, as the weeks passed, Mr. Grubbs became so
engrossed in watching Miss Penny's garden, that he quite forgot
about his own. He forgot to water. He forgot to weed.

"This is all *her* fault," he hissed, finding his pathetic
garden shriveled and dead.

By nightfall, Mr. Grubbs's anger had made him even more
determined. "Just so she doesn't win," he snarled, "that's all
that really matters."

But what mattered to Miss Penny was her garden. For forty-eight years she had tended turnips, cultivated carrots, and weeded watermelons. She was not about to give up now.

Miss Penny tried spraying her plants with an herbal mix called Rabbits Away, which the rabbits thought was quite tasty. Next she tried shining bright lights on the plants, leaving the sprinkler on at night, and putting sticky tape where paws might find it. She tried covering the plants with boxes, and blankets, and mosquito nets. In July, she even tried leaving out plates of store-bought vegetables so the rabbits might leave hers alone.

Miss Penny tried everything.

Then it all got out of hand. *More* hungry rabbits appeared.
Baby rabbits, too—more than even Mr. Grubbs could count.
"Eat up!" Mr. Grubbs chuckled. As the baby
rabbits quickly grew larger and larger, Miss Penny's
doomed garden grew smaller and smaller.

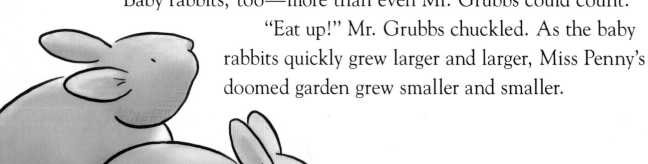

By summer's end, Miss Penny's garden was a nightmare.
Wearily she wandered down each row. Everything had been
nibbled, munched, crunched, and trampled. "I've had nothing
to give my friends," she moaned, "and now I have nothing for
the fair tomorrow."

Then something caught Miss Penny's eye—a sweet red
pepper. Somehow it had escaped the ravenous rabbits. It was
perfect, the most perfect pepper Miss Penny had ever seen.

"I will guard it myself," she cried excitedly, "all night.
And in the morning, I will take it to the fair."

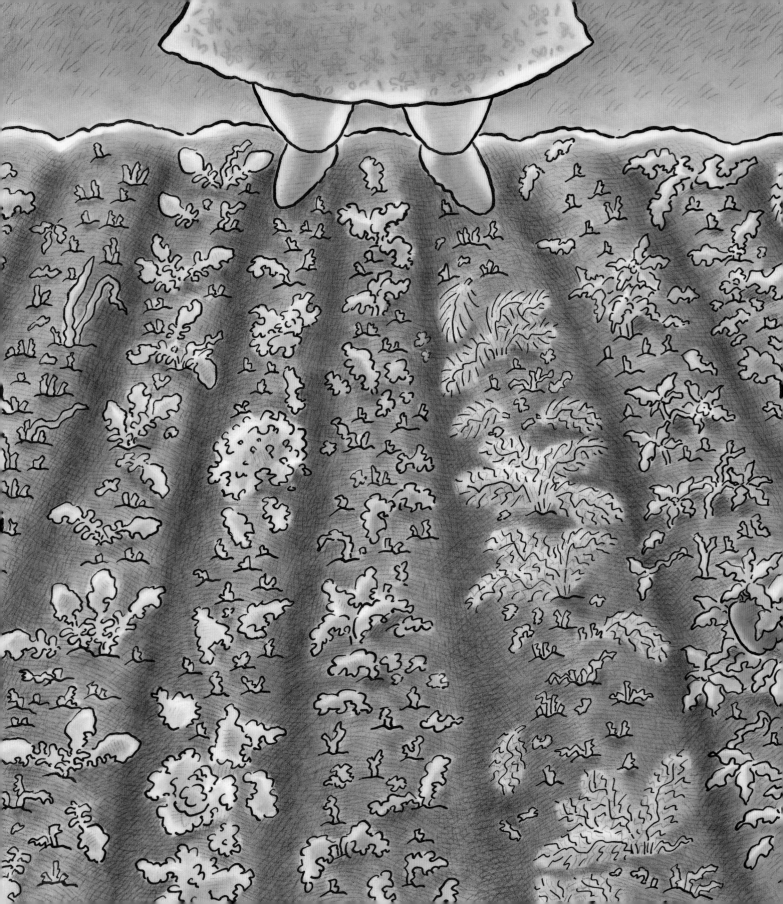

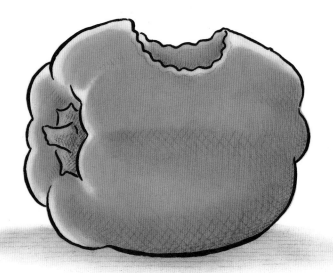

Miss Penny did, indeed, stay with her pepper all night long. But just before dawn, her eyes grew so heavy she could not keep them open.

The keen-eyed Mr. Grubbs saw his chance. Tiptoeing toward the rabbits, he hissed, "Go ahead, eat it!"

The rabbits refused to budge.

"Stupid animals," Mr. Grubbs sneered, plucking the prize pepper off of the plant himself. With a wicked smile, he took one bite of it, then dropped it on the ground.

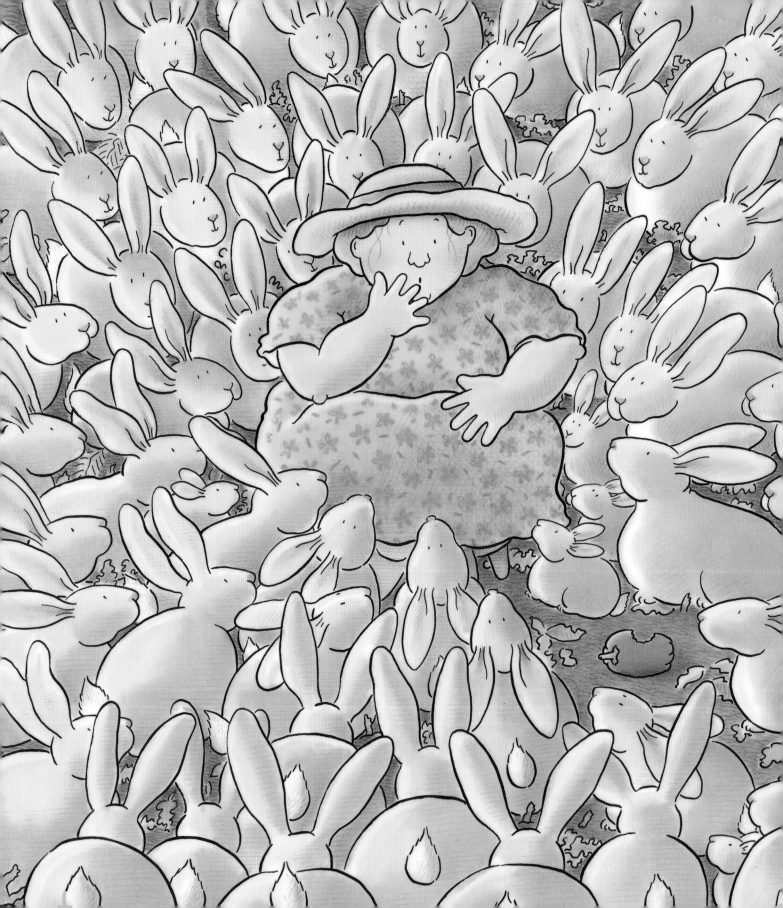

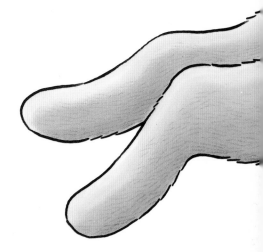

When Miss Penny woke up, she could not believe her eyes. Rabbits crowded all around her, and beside them lay the ruined pepper.

Miss Penny shook her head. "Now I have nothing for the fair," she cried. The rabbits—fat with glossy coats and shiny eyes—all twitched their noses.

Mr. Grubbs danced a victory jig in his backyard. At last, he had won!

Then, suddenly, he heard a noise. It was Miss Penny's truck driving off. Quickly peeking through the fence, Mr. Grubbs discovered that the rabbits, too, were gone.

Racing after the truck, Mr. Grubbs was shocked
to see it stop at the fairgrounds, and even more
surprised by the events that followed.

Miss Penny, with no vegetables, entered her
rabbits in the fair. Their incredible summer diet
had made them "spectacular examples of their
species" the judges said, awarding Miss Penny
top prizes.

And *after* the fair, Miss Penny delivered
gifts of rabbits to all of her friends.

The largest pair, she generously
saved for her long-time neighbor,
Mr. Grubbs.